DISNEY's

THE LITTLE MERMAID

THE PRACTICAL-JOKE WAR

by Stephanie St. Pierre

D1488039

DISNEY PRESS

NEW YORK

Look for all the books in this series:

Drawings by Philo Barnhart
Cover painting by Fred Marvin
Inking by Russell Spina, Jr.

ISBN: 1-56282-641-7

Disney's
THE LITTLE MERMAID

THE PRACTICAL-JOKE WAR

Ariel was running late as usual. She'd been out with her best friend, Flounder, looking for human treasures to add to the collection in her secret grotto. She hadn't found anything, but it had been fun swimming around the beautiful pink coral reefs. Long beams of late afternoon sunlight had streamed down through the water, lighting the coral in bright patches.

In fact, Ariel had been enjoying herself so much that she had completely lost track of time. Only her grumbling stomach had reminded her that it was almost dinnertime.

"Daddy is going to go crazy if I'm late for dinner," Ariel said, swimming as fast as she could.

"Why should today be any different?" joked Flounder.

"Very funny," said Ariel, giving his fin a tweak. "But I promised him I wouldn't be late for any more meals—at least this week. I just can't seem to keep my mind on the time. There are so many amazing and wonderful things to—

"Oh, look, who's that?" Ariel interrupted herself, pointing to an unusual-looking merwoman with flowing purple hair who had just swum into view. The woman had a large sack slung over her shoulder, and she was wearing a ragged robe that flowed out behind her as she moved through the water.

"That must be the old peddler woman," said Flounder. "Everyone in the kingdom has been talking about her. She travels around from one part of the ocean to another, buying, selling, and trading all kinds of stuff wherever she goes."

"How interesting!" Ariel gazed at the woman curiously, wondering what kinds of marvelous things she had in that sack. Maybe she had some human treasures! Almost without thinking, Ariel began to swim toward her.

Flounder hurried to catch up. "Ariel," he said warningly. "Don't forget—you're already late!"

Ariel reluctantly stopped swimming. "Oh, all right," she said with a sigh, gazing after the old merwoman. "I'll go straight home. But it looks as though she's headed out of the kingdom. I wish I'd had a chance to talk to her. Imagine the things she must have seen!" Ariel watched for a moment as the woman slowly drifted out of sight. Then she and Flounder hurried back to the palace.

"Good luck, Ariel," Flounder called out as Ariel raced through the castle door. She hurried through the pearly halls of the palace toward the royal dining hall. As she whizzed past the door to the throne room she was surprised to hear her father and Sebastian talking inside. Suddenly she remembered that her father wouldn't be joining them for dinner that evening. He was leaving the following morning on a trip that would keep him away from the kingdom for several days, and he had a lot of last-minute preparations to take care of. Ariel sighed with relief as she realized that for once she wouldn't be scolded for her tardiness.

I just hope my sisters haven't eaten everything already, Ariel thought to herself. She was about to round the corner and enter the hall when she heard the sound of loud, raucous laughter from within.

"What's going on in there?" she wondered aloud. She hurried to the doorway and paused for a moment, staring at the scene before her. Andrina was doubled over, laughing so hard that her face was turning bright red. Attina was nearly falling out of her chair. Even dignified Aquata was snorting with laughter.

Adella was the only one who wasn't laughing. She was sitting very still in front of her plate of seaweed salad with an annoyed expression on her face.

"What's so funny?" Ariel asked, swimming over to her place at the table. At least there's

4

still plenty of salad left, she thought.

Andrina tried to answer, but she couldn't stop laughing long enough to speak. Instead she just pointed at Adella and shook her head. Suddenly Adella smiled, and a twinkle came into her eye.

"Ariel, you *must* try this salad," she said sweetly. "It's a new recipe Andrina made up and it's . . . ," she giggled, ". . . well, it's absolutely unreal."

Ariel could tell that the rest of her sisters were trying hard to stifle their laughter, but she still couldn't see what was so funny. "OK," she said with a shrug, "I'll try the salad."

Adella quickly pushed her plate toward Ariel. "Here, you can have mine. I'm full," she said.

Ariel eyed the plate warily. It looked normal enough, but she was very suspicious now. Adella's appetite was legendary—in fact, Ariel couldn't ever remember hearing her claim to be full before! Ariel gingerly raised the plate and sniffed at the salad curiously.

"Oh, come on, Ariel. Just try it for goodness' sake," said Adella impatiently.

"All right," said Ariel. She popped a leaf into her mouth and chewed—and chewed and chewed and chewed!

"What is this stuff?" Ariel asked, still chewing. In reply, her sisters broke into new gales of laughter. Ariel finally gave up and carefully spit the unchewable seaweed into her napkin. "Yuck!" She poked at the lettuce with her finger. "It's made of rubber!" she exclaimed.

"Andrina is up to her usual tricks," said Adella haughtily.

"I should have known," Ariel said with a grin. Andrina was known throughout the kingdom as a notorious practical joker. "It tastes awful, but I must admit it's pretty funny."

"Adella actually ate a piece!" Andrina shrieked.

"I've always said that Adella will eat any-thing," Aquata commented. "Now we know it's true!"

"I did *not* eat it!" Adella cried. "I just chewed it for a very long time. I was trying to be polite, something the rest of you would

6

never think to do. Honestly, Andrina, you're so childish." Adella pushed herself away from the table and left the royal dining hall with a regal swish of her tail.

"She just can't take a joke," said Andrina with a giggle.

Ariel picked up another piece of the rubbery seaweed and flapped it back and forth. "Where in the seven seas did you get this stuff, anyway?" she asked.

"That's my little secret," said Andrina. "You know, I'm just full of surprises." And no matter how much her sisters pressed, that was all that Andrina would say on the matter. She ate quickly and excused herself before the others had finished. Ariel couldn't help noticing that Andrina had a strange gleam in her eyes. Now what is she up to? Ariel wondered.

* * *

After she left the table Andrina hurried to her room. She checked to be sure that none of her sisters had followed her, then locked the bedroom door. "Now to get down to business," she said, rubbing her hands together eagerly.

Earlier that day Andrina had gone out with some friends to see the peddler who had been wandering through the kingdom. Among the pretty shawls and shell jewelry the old woman had for sale, Andrina had discovered a real treasure. It was a small trunk filled with all kinds of props for playing jokes. Andrina had been so excited that she had bought the trunk and raced home with it just in time to play her first trick—the fake seaweed salad.

Along with the gadgets and gimmicks for practical jokes, the little trunk also contained a book that explained how to use the items and gave suggestions for new ways to play tricks. Andrina couldn't wait to try out every trick in the book.

She reached under her bed and pulled out the trunk. "That fake seaweed certainly livened up dinner today," she said to herself. Andrina laughed again at the memory of Adella's face as she chewed the rubbery salad. Then she rummaged through the trunk looking for another trick. "Now I think it's Aquata's turn," she decided.

Ariel had made plans to ride sea horses with her friend Coral after dinner. She was just leaving her room to go meet Coral when she saw Andrina sneaking into Aquata's bedroom.

"Hmmmm. I wonder what she's up to now?" Ariel said. She moved quietly toward the door of her oldest sister's room and peeked inside. Aquata's room was neat and perfectly beautiful. As usual, there wasn't a thing out of place. How could Andrina think anything she did in there would go unnoticed? Aquata was so particular about her things that she even noticed if someone sat on the bed and left it a tiny bit rumpled.

Then, as Ariel watched, Andrina set a beautiful crystal bottle decorated with a big purple bow on Aquata's dresser. A present? Ariel couldn't think of any reason why Andrina would be giving Aquata a gift. Maybe she's just being nice, Ariel thought, but I doubt it. I'll bet she's up to another one of her tricks. I wonder what the punch line to this one is.

Andrina turned around, and Ariel quickly dodged out of sight behind the door. She was so curious she could hardly stand it. She watched Andrina, who was smiling from ear to ear, come out of Aquata's room and disappear around the corner.

Ariel swam quickly through the palace and out toward the stables to meet Coral. As she swam she noticed that the water seemed a little rougher than usual. But she didn't think anything of it until she saw Coral waiting outside the stable with a disappointed look on her face.

"No riding today," Coral called out, swimming toward her friend. "A sea storm is brewing. Your father ordered the stables closed and everybody inside until it blows over."

"Oh dear," said Ariel. "It's a good thing he's not leaving on his trip until tomorrow morning. I hope it blows over soon."

"Oh, it'll probably clear up within a few hours," said Coral. "Unfortunately for us, though, it'll be too late to ride by then."

"Why don't you come back to the palace," Ariel suggested. "I'm sure we can find something to do inside." Her blue eyes sparkled. "I have a feeling something interesting might happen soon." She quickly filled her friend in on what had happened at dinner that day. She also told her about seeing Andrina in Aquata's room.

"What do you think is in the bottle?" Coral asked as the two mermaids swam back toward the palace.

Ariel shrugged. "Knowing Andrina, it could be anything," she said. "Come on, let's hurry. I want to be around when Aquata finds it."

Ariel and Coral sped up and soon reached the palace. They swam inside and were halfway down the hall to Ariel's room when they heard a piercing scream.

"Uh-oh," said Ariel with a grin. "I think we're too late. That sounded like Aquata. Let's go!" The mermaids raced to Aquata's room. They got there at the same time as Andrina, Arista, and Adella did, and hurried through the door after them.

"Look at me!" cried Aquata as they entered. "What am I going to do?" Aquata was sitting in front of her fancy dressing table, wearing a gorgeous pink pearl and scallop-shell necklace. Her hair was twisted on top of her head with more pearls carefully wound through it. She looked beautiful except for one thing: her face was smeared with dark purple streaks! "I'm supposed to see my date in half an hour. I can't believe it. How could this happen?"

"Oh dear," Andrina said. "You poor thing. Whatever did you put on your face?" Ariel could have sworn that Andrina was choking back a chuckle.

"I thought it was a present from my

boyfriend, Nexar. It was here when I came in, wrapped up with this big bow." A big fat tear left a streak down Aquata's purple cheek. "I thought it was so nice. I rubbed it on. And then I looked in the mirror . . . and my face . . ." Aquata broke into loud sobs.

"Oh, don't be such a crybaby," said Andrina. "It's just a joke." Everyone turned and stared at her. "Well, look at her," said Andrina defensively. "She does look funny, doesn't she?" At first no one laughed. Then a giggle started slipping out here and there as the other mermaids realized that Andrina was right. Aquata *did* look pretty funny.

"Stop it, all of you!" cried Aquata. "It's not funny. I look hideous."

"Don't worry; it comes off," Andrina said, holding out another small bottle of lotion. "Here, use this."

"Why should I?" Aquata demanded with a sniffle.

"Because it will take away the stains," said Andrina, exasperated.

Aquata tried a tiny bit of the lotion on her chin, which quickly returned to its normal color. Then, satisfied that Andrina

wasn't playing another joke, Aquata rubbed the lotion all over her face until the purple stains were gone. "Much better," she said with relief.

"Oh, I don't know about that," said Andrina with a giggle.

"*You* can leave now," Aquata said to her coldly.

"Oh, come on—it was just a joke," Andrina said. "Can't you take a joke?"

"You seemed to think Andrina had a better sense of humor at dinnertime," Adella reminded Aquata. "You were laughing pretty hard when the joke was on *me*."

"Well, that was different," Aquata said. "At least your face didn't turn purple. Frankly, Andrina, I think you're getting too funny for your own good. Now everybody out. I'll have to hurry if I want to be ready in time for my date." She got up and shooed her sisters and Coral out of the room. "And Andrina," she added, "I'll get you back for this. I promise." Then she slammed her door.

"Yipes," said Ariel. She hated it when her sisters were angry.

"It *was* kind of funny," whispered Coral.

"Shhh," said Ariel. She tugged her friend along to her own room. As soon as the door was shut behind them the two girls collapsed on Ariel's bed and burst out laughing.

But suddenly Coral stopped laughing. Her eyes widened, and her face paled.

"What's wrong?" Ariel asked anxiously.

"Ariel!" Coral gasped. She pointed with a shaking finger at a chair in the corner of Ariel's room. "Do you see what I see?"

"Uh-oh!" Ariel gulped. A long, spiky leg was sticking out from behind the chair. There was a dangerous-looking pincer at the end of it. It could belong to only one thing—a spider crab.

"What are we going to do?" squealed Coral. "I hate those things more than anything! They're so gross!"

"Calm down, Coral," said Ariel. "You know it's not going to hurt us."

"But what if it pinches us or gets into our hair?" Coral cried. "Ugh! I think I'd die!"

"Just relax," said Ariel in what she hoped was a soothing voice. She grabbed a pillow from her bed. "You open the door and

17

stand back. I'll scare it out from behind the chair."

"You want *me* to go right past it to open the door?" Coral screeched in horror. "No way! I don't want to go anywhere near that thing!"

"Come on," said Ariel. "We'll chase it outside where it belongs. After all, it's probably more afraid of us than we are of it, right?"

"Don't bet on it," Coral muttered. But she sidled toward the door, moving her fins as little as possible to avoid drawing the creature's attention.

"Ready?" Ariel asked when the door was open. She inched her way over toward the leg, holding the pillow high. She nudged the chair with the tip of her tail. Then she started to laugh.

"What is it?" Coral cried in a panicked voice. "Did it bite you? What's wrong, Ariel?"

Ariel leaned down and grabbed the leg as Coral gasped in horror. "Don't worry, Coral," she said. "There's no spider crab at all! It's just a leg."

"It's fake?" Coral exclaimed, slumping against the door in relief.

"Andrina strikes again," Ariel said, shaking her head.

"I wonder where Andrina is," Ariel commented the next morning. She and all her other sisters were eating breakfast in the royal dining hall.

"She's probably plotting some new practical joke," said Adella. "I just hope I'm not one of her victims today."

"I know what you mean. I don't think Coral will be coming over for a while," said Ariel. "Not after the joke Andrina played on us yesterday." She told the others about the fake spider crab.

"That's nothing compared to what she did to me," said Attina. "When I opened my desk drawer a smelly, smoky cloud exploded out of it. It was as dark as squid ink, but it smelled totally disgusting. My whole room was full of it for the rest of the afternoon." Attina wrinkled her nose at the memory.

"Hmmm," Ariel said. "I'd like to know where she's coming up with these tricks."

"Well, I'd like to put a stop to them," Adella declared. "They're beginning to make me nervous."

"It is getting a little tiresome, isn't it?" said Alana.

"Definitely," Aquata agreed wholeheartedly. "Somebody needs to teach Andrina a lesson."

Arista smiled. "Oh, come on, you guys. Don't be such bad sports. It's not as if Andrina has done anything really horrible."

"You wouldn't say that if *your* face had turned purple," Aquata replied. But Ariel noticed that her oldest sister was looking more thoughtful than angry.

"What are you thinking about, Aquata?" Ariel asked.

Aquata raised one eyebrow. "I'm just trying to figure out my revenge," she replied with a smile. "I vowed to get her back, remember?"

"Revenge?" Alana said nervously. "That doesn't sound like such a good idea to me. Maybe if we just ignore Andrina's jokes, she'll get tired of them."

"Not a chance," Attina said. "When Andrina gets like this there's no stopping her."

"Right," said Aquata. "The only way to get her to leave us alone is to play a really good joke on *her*."

"Aquata's right," said Adella. "That way at least we'll get to have the last laugh for a change. Can anybody think of a good joke to play?"

"Shush," said Ariel. "Here she comes." The sisters all quickly pretended to concentrate on their breakfasts. Nobody looked up when Andrina came in.

Andrina stifled a yawn as she sat down in her chair. "I guess I overslept," she said.

"Did your guilty conscience keep you up?" asked Aquata.

Andrina laughed. "Oh, Aquata, get over it already. It's not as if your face stayed purple or anything. Why should I feel guilty?"

"Well, I just hope you have the good sense not to try anything like that on me again," Aquata said.

"Relax," said Andrina. "It's not much fun to play jokes on somebody who's so fussy anyway. Now Ariel, on the other hand, has an excellent sense of humor. . . ."

"True," said Ariel. "But I've also got to get to school. I'm supposed to meet with Mr. Chubb before class to talk about my science project, and I'm sure he won't have much of a sense of humor if I'm late. See you all later." She grabbed her schoolbag and hurried out. Flounder was waiting near the castle gate to swim along with her.

"So, what's new at the palace?" he asked.

"Well, Andrina's still up to her usual tricks," said Ariel. She told him about her sister's latest practical jokes. "I think she's plotting another one for me now. To tell you the truth, I'm kind of looking forward to it. She's got some really cool props. I wish I knew where she got them." Ariel chuckled, remembering the look on Aquata's purple-streaked face. "I can't imagine what she has in store for me."

"I'm sure you'll find out soon enough."

"True." Ariel had reached the school. "See you later, Flounder." She waved good-bye and headed inside.

* * *

Meanwhile, Aquata had also left the palace and was swimming toward the main part of town as fast as she could. She knew she'd have to hurry if she didn't want to be late for school, but she really wanted to get her errand done that morning. She giggled to herself as she swam, thinking about the plot she'd hatched up to get back at Andrina. She hadn't told her sisters about it at breakfast because she wanted to make sure it was a surprise for Andrina—she didn't want any of the others to accidentally let something slip and give it away.

Soon she reached the royal theater. She

went inside and discovered that the usual Friday morning rehearsal was already in progress, just as she'd hoped. The theater troupe was practicing a new musical called *Catfish*. Normally Aquata loved to sit and watch them; she enjoyed seeing the actors rehearse their big song-and-dance numbers, try on costumes, recite their lines—anything that had to do with the theater fascinated her.

But today she had other things on her mind, and she hardly glanced at the actors onstage before hurrying backstage. Her new boyfriend, a young merman named Nexar, had recently started working at the theater as a junior stagehand. She soon found him in the wings working on a piece of scenery.

"Aquata!" he exclaimed when he saw her. "What are you doing here?" He smiled and swam over to meet her.

"I have a favor to ask," she told him breathlessly. "I need to borrow an actor."

He looked surprised. But she began whispering rapidly in his ear, explaining what she had planned. When she finished, Nexar laughed. "I'll see what I can do," he promised. "Stop by here after school, and we'll work out the details."

"Great!" Aquata exclaimed. "I knew I could count on you." As she rushed off toward school, Aquata grinned with excitement. She could hardly wait!

4

In science class that day, Ariel and Coral sat
with Ariel's cousin Marlon and their friend
Gil. The four of them were working on their
group science project together. They had
been studying the life cycle of the brine
shrimp for several weeks. At their meeting
that morning their teacher, Mr. Chubb, had
told them that they should be prepared to
give their oral report the following Tuesday.
So now they were going over the notes they
had all been taking and planning what

27

diagrams and drawings to include in their presentation.

"OK, so whose turn is it to take home these weird little creatures this weekend?" asked Coral. "I've had enough of them, and I've done my part graphing their growth rate."

"I think the only one who hasn't taken them yet is Ariel," said Gil.

"You're right. I'll take them," Ariel said. "Hey, maybe I can think of a way to scare Andrina with them. They *are* pretty gross looking."

"I doubt it," said Coral with a laugh. "Andrina doesn't scare that easily. So what's she done lately?"

Ariel quickly filled the boys in on Andrina's jokes and then described the smelly smoke trick she'd played on Attina.

"You should think of something to do to get back at her," said Gil.

"That's what Aquata says. But the thing is, Andrina has all these great props," said Ariel. "And we don't know where she found them."

"I'll bet I know," said Marlon.

"Really?" said Ariel. "Where?"

"The old peddler woman," Marlon replied. "She had all kinds of stuff she was trying to sell and trade. One of the things was this old trunk full of little bottles and gadgets and fake seaweed and stuff like that. Andrina must have bought the trunk."

"Wow," said Ariel. "I'd like to get my hands on that trunk for a while. At least then I might have a fighting chance."

"What do you mean?" asked Coral.

"I think Andrina's planning to play another joke on me today."

"Well, school's almost over," said Gil. "So I guess you're about to find out."

"You're right." Ariel sighed. "But in the meantime we've still got two charts to make before the end of class." She didn't think she'd ever want to hear another thing about brine shrimp in her whole life once this project was finished. Still, she comforted herself with the thought that it was almost over. When Mr. Chubb said it was time to go home, Ariel put her books into her schoolbag and tucked the jar of brine shrimp in on top of them.

"Hi, Ariel!" called Flounder. He had been waiting for Ariel just outside the school doors. "You have to come with me! I've got a surprise for you." With that, he took off in a flurry of fins and tail.

"Flounder, slow down," cried Ariel, swimming after him. "What's your hurry?" she asked as she caught up.

"Wait until you see it," said Flounder. He seemed so excited that Ariel was getting really curious. "I can't tell you anything else or it'll ruin the surprise."

"OK," said Ariel. "You've got me now." She loved surprises. Flounder smiled and quickened his pace even more, swimming along the path Ariel usually took home from school. However, he didn't stop at the palace. Instead, he swam on past it until he reached a rocky cove.

The steep walls of the cove were covered with seaweed, sponges, and colorful sea anemones. They surrounded the cove on all sides except for a narrow opening. Flounder swam through the opening, with Ariel right behind him. Far above them the walls came close together almost like a roof, making the cove seem dark and mysterious.

"OK, Flounder," Ariel said, "let's see the big surprise."

"Ta-da!" Flounder swirled in a circle above a small mound in the sand.

"What is it?" asked Ariel, confused.

"It's a treasure," said Flounder. "Now you have to dig it up." Flounder swam down and nudged at the mound eagerly, dislodging the object a little so that a piece of its shiny surface glittered in the dark water.

"How did you find it?" asked Ariel.

"This angelfish I know dared me to swim in here," Flounder explained. "She didn't think I'd be brave enough, but I was—even though she said there might be barracudas." He gulped at the memory. "When I swam in I saw this funny lump here in the sand. I was sure it must be buried treasure, so I decided to wait for you so we could dig it up together."

As Ariel brushed the sand away from the object she saw that it was a huge glittering jewel. "It's incredible," she said, picking it up. "I wonder where it came from. It doesn't look as though it's been buried for very long at all."

"What's that on the side?" Flounder asked.

"I don't know," said Ariel. She turned the jewel sideways to look at the small button Flounder had noticed. "But we should try to find out if anyone lost it. It looks valuable." She turned the jewel upright and pressed the little button. Suddenly the top of the jewel flew off, and three enormous green-and-black spotted eels flew out at her!

Ariel screamed. Flounder darted behind her in fear. "Help! Save us!" he shrieked. The eels writhed around wildly for a moment. Then they began to sink.

"Hey, wait a second," said Ariel. Her heart was still pounding, but as the eels slowly sank and lay motionless on the sand she saw that they weren't real. Just then she heard laughter from outside the entrance to the grotto. "Andrina!" she cried, shaking her head. She looked at Flounder, who had covered his eyes with his fins. "It's OK,

Flounder. It was just another one of Andrina's practical jokes."

"It was a joke?" Flounder asked weakly. He uncovered his eyes, but he was still shaking.

"Uh-huh. Could that have been the angelfish who dared you to come in here?" Ariel asked him, pointing toward the opening of the grotto where a little angelfish was swimming in circles and laughing hard. A moment later Andrina peeked through the opening, a big grin on her face. She waved at Ariel, then swam away, laughing all the while. Ariel shook her head and chuckled despite herself. It *was* kind of funny, now that she'd caught her breath again. She bent down to retrieve her schoolbag, which she'd dropped in all the excitement. That was when she noticed that the jar that had contained the brine shrimp was lying, empty, on the sand. "Oh no!" she gasped.

"What?" asked Flounder, looking around nervously as if expecting more eels to spring out of nowhere.

"Look," Ariel said, holding up the empty

jar. "My science experiment got away." She stared at the jar in her hand. She could hardly believe that the brine shrimp she and her classmates had tended so carefully for weeks had escaped into the vast sea. "What am I going to tell Coral and Gil and Marlon on Monday?"

"I'm sorry," said Flounder, hanging his head. "I guess I brought you right into a trap."

"It's not your fault," said Ariel. "You didn't know." She gave her friend a hug. Then she put the empty jar back into her schoolbag and picked up the fake eels. They had springs inside their long bodies, so it was easy to squish them up and stuff them back into the jewel.

Ariel sat down on a rock and sighed. "I can't believe my whole science project is ruined," she said. "What am I going to do? We've been working on it for weeks. My friends are going to be so mad at me, and it's all Andrina's fault. Why does she have to get so carried away with these jokes?"

"I could try to collect some new brine shrimp for you," Flounder offered.

"Thanks, Flounder," said Ariel sadly. "But we have to keep track of how they grow from the time they hatch until the end of the experiment. There's nothing to do but start the whole thing over."

"We could go look for some new brine-shrimp eggs, then," Flounder suggested.

"No, that's OK. I'll do it later." Ariel tossed the fake jewel into her schoolbag. "You know, this might all have been funny if it hadn't been for the brine shrimp escaping."

"I didn't think it was funny," said Flounder. "I don't like eels. They bite."

"Silly guppy," said Ariel. She smiled at her friend and got up. "We'd better get moving. It *won't* be funny if I'm late for music class again. Sebastian was so angry the last time that I was sure he'd talk to Daddy about it. Besides, I don't want to spend any more time right now thinking about how mad my friends are going to be about the science project." She sighed, remembering all the hard work they'd put into it. She couldn't imagine what Mr. Chubb was going to say when she told him what had happened.

"What are you going to do about Andrina?" asked Flounder.

"Well, at least now I know where she's getting all those great props," Ariel said. She smiled grimly. "And one good joke deserves another. I've just got to find a way to get into that trunk!"

Ariel rushed into the music room a moment before Sebastian arrived. She had just enough time to get out her music and settle into her seat before he began tapping his baton to get the sisters' attention.

"Andrina told us all about her latest little joke," Adella whispered to Ariel. "Did *you* think it was funny?"

"Well, I might have, except that my science project got ruined, and now Coral and Gil and Marlon are going to kill me," Ariel whispered back.

"Quiet!" commanded Sebastian. "We have a most important program to prepare for," he began. "Your father has invited some of the most important people in the kingdom to a dinner party next week, when he returns from his visit to the Arctic Ocean. You will be performing for them before dinner, and I want all of you to be prepared. Is that understood?"

The sisters nodded and promised they would do their best. They all knew how nervous Sebastian was before a big concert.

"Unfortunately, Octavio has a cold, so he won't be able to accompany us today. I expect you to sing all the louder to make up for his absence."

As Sebastian droned on about the program, Adella passed Ariel a note. Ariel unfolded it and read:

Pretend to sing when Sebastian gives the signal, but don't make a sound! Pass it on.

Ariel stifled a giggle. She knew it had to be another one of Andrina's crazy ideas and that they probably shouldn't encourage her.

Still, Ariel couldn't resist playing such a harmless little trick on Sebastian, especially when he was being so stern and serious.

"All right, girls." Sebastian tapped his baton again. "Are you ready? We will begin with the first measure on page ten in your books." Sebastian counted out the beat and began to conduct. The sisters mouthed the words just as if they were singing, but not a sound came out of their mouths. Sebastian continued to conduct for a few bars before he realized what was—or rather what wasn't—happening.

He stopped suddenly. So did the sisters. Sebastian glared at them suspiciously, then tapped his baton again. "Now let's try it again, and no silliness. Sing *out loud.*" He counted out the beat again.

As Sebastian began counting, Andrina whispered something to Attina, who quickly passed the message along to Alana. Soon all the sisters had heard the new plan. As Sebastian counted the final beat they were ready. They let loose singing as loudly as they possibly could. Sebastian was so shocked he nearly fell off his podium. The girls tried hard not to laugh at the expression on Sebastian's face. As soon as he regained his composure his red shell began to glow brighter than ever, and he glared at the princesses angrily. He didn't seem amused at the joke they'd played on him.

"Enough, enough!" he cried. "Why, if your father were here, I'd . . . No more practice today! You girls are too much. I need a vacation!" With that, Sebastian dropped his baton and scuttled out of the music room. As soon as he was gone the girls howled with laughter.

"Now *that* was funny," Adella gasped between her giggles.

Finally the girls stopped laughing, collected their things, and headed back toward their rooms. Everyone had to admit that Andrina's idea had been terrific. But as Andrina swam away ahead of them into her own room and locked the door, the other princesses couldn't help wondering what she might be plotting next.

"I hear you were treated to one of Andrina's special jokes today," Aquata said to Ariel.

"An exploding jewel full of eels," said Ariel.

"Well, tonight at dinner Andrina will get a taste of her own medicine," said Aquata.

"What do you mean?" asked Ariel.

"Are you playing a joke on Andrina?" Adella exclaimed.

"You'll see," Aquata replied smugly. She smiled and slipped into her own bedroom.

"I wonder what Aquata has planned," said Alana.

"I guess we'll know at dinner," said Ariel. She shook her head. "Things sure are getting crazy around here."

The sisters sat quietly at the dinner table that evening. They were all wondering if Andrina would play another joke during the meal. They were also curious about what Aquata had planned.

"So, don't you have anything to amuse us with tonight, Andrina?" Adella asked.

"Even *I* need a break from so much laughing," said Andrina. "My stomach still aches from this afternoon."

"I just hope Sebastian doesn't tell Father when he gets back from his trip," said Alana.

"Don't be such a worrywart," Andrina said. "Sebastian will forget all about it by tomorrow morning. He's got more important things to think about than one silly joke."

"I'm not so sure about that," said Ariel. "Sometimes you can just go too far. Like when you ruined my science project."

"I thought we were talking about Sebastian," said Andrina. "He *will* forget about what happened today. No harm was done. We just missed one practice. We'll have plenty of time to make up for it before we have to perform."

"That's true," said Alana. "But what about Ariel's project? If you hadn't played that trick on her, she wouldn't have lost her brine shrimp. It's your fault that she's going to have to do the whole thing over."

"Well, of course I'm sorry that happened," said Andrina impatiently. "But I think you're all being a little unfair. I didn't mean to ruin her project. . . ."

"Excuse me, Princess Andrina, but you have a visitor," announced Dover, the palace butler, coming into the room.

"Who is it?" Andrina asked.

"I'm afraid I don't know, Princess," the butler replied. "The young gentleman refused to give his name, but he insisted I interrupt Your Highness right now to announce him." Dover shook his head in dismay. "Most irregular, I must say. *Most* irregular."

"Why don't you invite this young gentleman in so that we can all meet him, Andrina," Aquata suggested.

"Why not?" Andrina said. "Show him in, please, Dover." The butler swam out of the room and returned a moment later followed by a young man dressed in a ridiculous costume. His face was painted like a clown's, and he wore a big red nose and a purple wig. Around his neck was a huge white ruffled collar. He began juggling as he entered.

"Ah, the fair Princess Andrina," the young man said, continuing to juggle as he bowed to her. "Word has traveled far and wide of your great talents. And now, as a representative of the finest jokesters in the sea, I would like to officially welcome you to our ranks. A princess in our midst makes us all more noble. We are truly grateful that you have taken up our cause."

"And what cause is that?" asked Andrina, looking curious and amused.

"Why, the cause of practical jokes," replied the clown. "The cause of keeping everyone in the kingdom on their tails. Everyone has been talking about it. You may be a princess here in the palace. But I have come tonight to tell you that among clowns, you are a queen."

Andrina's sisters began to giggle.

"Queen of the Clowns!" exclaimed Arista. "It's perfect!"

"And to show you how much we appreciate you," the clown continued, "we have a special gift for you." He turned and reached into a large box that Dover had just carried into the room.

"Oh, a present," Andrina said happily. "Let me have it!"

"I certainly will," said the clown, reaching

into the box. Then he turned around and threw a sea-foam pie at Andrina! It landed on her face with a splat.

"How dare you," Andrina sputtered, wiping the foam from her face. "I should call the palace guards!"

"It is an honor to have you as our queen," the clown said. He bowed deeply, then ducked as Andrina threw a handful of sea-foam pie at him.

"Maybe you should leave," suggested Aquata, "before the queen loses her temper." The clown winked at Aquata and left the room, laughing. "What's the matter, Andrina," said Aquata between giggles, "can't you take a joke?"

"A joke?" said Andrina. She began to smile, then to laugh. "And who is the mastermind behind this joke, Aquata—you?"

"I only wanted to see if you could still laugh when the joke was on you," said Aquata. "Can you?"

"Oh . . ." Andrina looked around at her sisters, who were all still laughing. "Sure, why not." Andrina picked up a handful of sea foam and threw it at Aquata. It landed in Aquata's lap with a splat.

"Hey!" Aquata scooped up the pie and threw it back, but she missed and the pie hit Attina. Suddenly sea-foam pie was flying everywhere. Finally, worn out, laughing, and completely messy, the mermaids headed for bed.

"Aquata, you've created a monster," said Ariel. It was Sunday evening, and all the sisters except Andrina had gathered in Adella's room to talk before bed.

"I'm afraid my little joke only encouraged her," agreed Aquata. Beginning on Saturday morning, everywhere the sisters turned they discovered surprises that Andrina had left for them. And all weekend long the sound of Andrina's laughter had floated through the palace.

"She must be getting up awfully early to plant all those tricks," said Adella.

"I'm starting to get a little tired of Andrina's sense of humor," said Alana. "This morning I washed my hands with soap that turned them black. It took me half an hour to get them clean again."

"At least you didn't get any of that horrible gum she gave me yesterday," said Attina. "I still can't get the taste of it out of my mouth. Yuck!"

"If you think that's bad, you should have tasted the hot-sea-pepper toothpaste she left me," said Arista, making a face.

"Why has Andrina gone totally crazy with these jokes?" asked Attina.

Ariel shrugged. "I don't know. And I don't know how we can get her to stop, unless we can get that trunk away from her."

"What trunk?" asked Arista curiously.

Ariel told them about the trunk that Marlon had seen the peddler trying to sell. "I think Andrina bought the trunk, and that's where she's been getting all this joke stuff. I mean, she's always played jokes on us, but the trunk has got to be the reason she's so out of control with them now."

"And if we could get it away from her . . . ," Arista began.

"She couldn't use that stuff on us anymore!" said Adella.

"Right," said Ariel.

"Maybe we should just tell Father," suggested Alana. "He'll be back in two days. He could put a stop to this nonsense right away."

"There's got to be a better way," said Ariel.

"Ariel's right. I'd hate to bother Father with this," said Aquata.

"Me, too," said Ariel. "But if I bite into one more piece of fake seaweed salad or weirdly flavored candy, I'm going to scream! It's getting so I'm afraid to eat."

"I know what you mean," said Attina. "This morning when I opened my closet a big black sea snake popped out at me. It wasn't real, of course, but it nearly scared me to death."

"None of you have had that creepy fake sea slug on your pillow yet, have you? That's the worst trick of all, as far as I'm concerned," said Arista. "It's so slimy."

"We have to think of something," said Ariel. "Tomorrow after school let's meet to come up with a plan for curing our sister of her practical joking."

"And if all else fails, we'll just have to tell Father," said Aquata. The other mermaids nodded in agreement. As they went off to bed they all watched carefully for more of Andrina's tricks.

"She must have finally gotten worn out and had enough for the day," muttered Ariel to herself when she reached her room. "Or maybe not." Ariel sighed and stared at the big ugly sea slug on her pillow. She knew it was fake, but it was still disgusting looking. She knocked the sea slug to the floor, flipped over her pillow, and went to bed. It had been a long day.

8

The next morning Ariel woke up late. Her other sisters had already left for school by the time she sat down to eat breakfast. She hurried through her meal, grabbed her schoolbag, and swam out of the palace as fast as she could. She was dreading having to explain to Gil, Marlon, and Coral about the brine shrimp, but she was dreading explaining it to Mr. Chubb even more. She knew he was going to be terribly disappointed in her for messing up the project, and her being late to school certainly wasn't going to make him any happier. Ariel put on an extra burst of speed and swam smack into Alana as she rounded a patch of seaweed.

"Oh, Ariel, it was terrible," gasped Alana. "The most awful thing . . ."

"Alana, what's wrong?" Ariel asked. Alana was crying hard. She looked terribly upset.

"It's Andrina," said Alana. "She told me my oysters were sick. My poor little oysters that never did a thing to her at all."

Ariel gasped. "She didn't hurt them, did she?" Ariel knew that Andrina had gotten out of hand with her practical jokes, but she couldn't believe her sister would harm innocent creatures just for a laugh.

"N-no, they're all right," said Alana, still sobbing. "But when she told me they were sick I was so worried I didn't know what to do. I hurried to them and found one out of its bed. When I picked it up to see if it was OK, it opened and *squirted* me in the face. It wasn't a real oyster at all—it was just another one of Andrina's horrible jokes! Oh, Ariel, how *could* she?" With that, Alana swam

away toward the palace. Ariel didn't know what to do. Should she follow Alana home or go to school?

"She didn't take that very well," said Andrina a bit sheepishly. She had been hiding behind a clump of seaweed, but now she poked her head out to talk to Ariel.

"That was a really awful thing to do," Ariel said angrily. "You know how Alana is about those oysters. How could you scare her like that? Don't you see that it wasn't a bit funny?" She stared at Andrina. All the sisters knew how sensitive Alana was when it came to the sea creatures she lovingly cared for. How could Andrina have been so cruel?

"Don't tell me *you're* upset about those dumb oysters, too," Andrina said. "I didn't do anything to them. I didn't even touch them. Look." She held out the fake oyster. Ariel reached out a finger and tapped its shell.

"Hey!" she cried as the oyster suddenly opened and squirted out a jet of green foam. Ariel tried to duck out of the way, but she was too slow. Now she had a big blob of green foam in her hair. Andrina started laughing.

"Isn't that great?" she exclaimed. Andrina tapped the oyster shell again and laughed as it squirted another jet of green foam.

Ariel just shook her head. "To tell you the truth, I'm getting sick of your dumb jokes," she said.

"It's just supposed to be fun," said Andrina. "Ariel, I know you're still mad about what happened the other day. I'm really sorry about your experiment. Listen, I'll help you redo it, OK?"

"You can't just apologize and make it all better," Ariel replied as she tried to clean the foam out of her hair. "Yuck, what a mess. Now thanks to you I'm going to be late for school, too."

"Come on, Ariel," Andrina said. "Can't you take a little joke? I didn't mean any harm. . . ."

"Andrina, you're really too much," said Ariel.

She swam away angrily. Her sister had really gone overboard with this trick, she thought. Had Andrina totally lost the ability to tell what was funny and what was just plain mean?

* * *

Ariel was still angry when she got to school. She arrived just as Mr. Chubb was calling the class to order. He told the students to break into their usual study groups to read and discuss that day's history assignment. Ariel grabbed her history book and swam over to where Coral, Gil, and Marlon were sitting. Even though she knew she had to tell her friends about the brine shrimp, she couldn't help complaining about Andrina first.

"Gee," Coral said. "That trick with the oysters was pretty mean. Alana gets so worked up about that kind of thing."

"Yeah, but the squirting oyster sounds cool," Gil commented.

Ariel shot him a disapproving look. "It would be cool if she didn't use it on such a softshell," she said. "It's not that the tricks and jokes are so bad themselves. Some of them are really pretty funny. It's just that Andrina can't seem to stop. And she doesn't

seem to think about who might get hurt."
Ariel gulped nervously. "That reminds me:
I've got some really bad news." She told her
friends about the brine shrimp.

"I can't believe it!" cried Coral.

"That's it," said Marlon. "I say we give
Andrina a taste of what it's like to be on the
other end of a joke."

"Oh, we tried that already," Ariel said.
She was just beginning to explain Aquata's
Queen of the Clowns trick when Mr. Chubb
called on their group. They were totally
unprepared.

"Uh-oh," whispered Coral. "Does anybody know anything at all about the history
of the Mediterranean Crustacean Congress
of 1174?"

"Yikes," Ariel whispered back. She cleared
her throat. "Um, Mr. Chubb, could I talk to
you privately for a minute?"

The teacher looked surprised. "Can't it
wait, Ariel? We're in the middle of a lesson."

"That's partly what I want to talk to you
about," Ariel explained meekly.

"Well, all right," Mr. Chubb said. "Class,

continue reading in your textbooks for a few minutes." He gestured for Ariel to come up to his desk.

As she got up from her seat, Ariel leaned over to Coral. "Since it's my fault we've been talking about Andrina rather than history, I'll explain to Mr. Chubb why we don't have an answer," she whispered quickly. "And while I'm at it, I might as well tell him why we won't have a science project for the oral report tomorrow." She left her friends and swam up to the teacher's desk. They spoke quietly for a few moments. Mr. Chubb glanced over at the others and frowned.

"Well, Ariel," he said finally. "Perhaps you had better go see Ms. Finn about this matter after class today. And I expect all four of you to be ready to give your report as soon as you can re-create the experiment."

"Yes, Mr. Chubb," said Ariel. She returned to her seat, and the teacher called on the next group.

"Are you OK?" Coral asked.

"Great," Ariel whispered. "Now I've got to go to the principal's office. And I can thank Andrina for that, too."

"Don't worry, Ariel," said Gil, who had been whispering with Marlon. "We've got something planned that'll put a stop to that pesky sister of yours."

"Let's talk about it after school," Ariel said with a sigh.

As soon as class was over, Ariel packed up her schoolbag and went to see Ms. Finn.

"Now, Ariel," the principal began, "just because you are a princess, you mustn't think that gives you special privileges. In fact, I think that is all the more reason for you to behave in a most impeccable manner, to set an example to the other young people in the kingdom. You know they look up to you princesses."

"Yes, Ms. Finn," said Ariel obediently. As Ms. Finn talked on and on, Ariel looked around the office and wondered how the many precarious stacks of papers piled everywhere stayed upright. The piles all seemed to be about to collapse, making the whole office look off-balance.

"Ariel, are you listening?" Ms. Finn looked directly at her.

"Yes, Ms. Finn," Ariel lied. "I just have a

lot on my mind," she added more truthfully. "You know, I've got that science project to redo. I was just thinking about that."

"Well . . ." Ms. Finn seemed uncertain whether or not to let Ariel go. "I suppose I've made my point," she said at last.

"Oh yes, indeed," Ariel said. Before Ms. Finn could change her mind, Ariel picked up her schoolbag and headed for the door. "Thank you so much," she said as she left the office. "I'll think about what you said."

Ariel swam to Coral's house, where her friends were waiting for her. After such a crummy day Ariel was glad to have the chance to think about something fun for a while.

"Listen to the plan these guys have come up with," Coral said excitedly. "It's great!"

"OK, let's hear it," said Ariel.

"Well," said Gil, "Marlon was talking about how we should do something that would force Andrina to give up the trunk."

"Then she couldn't keep playing jokes on everybody," said Marlon.

"And we could use some of that stuff ourselves," added Gil. "I can just hear my sister screaming when she finds a sea slug in her jewelry box!" Marlon and Gil started laughing.

Ariel rolled her eyes. "So tell me the plan."

"First we'll need a wig," said Gil.

"And some fancy robes," said Marlon.

"And how about a wand?" added Coral. The boys nodded in agreement.

"What do you need all that stuff for?" asked Ariel.

"For the magician!" Marlon and Gil said together.

"What magician?"

"The magician who has come to find his stolen trunk," said Marlon.

"But you can't accuse the old peddler woman of stealing," said Ariel.

"OK," said Gil. "We'll say that someone else stole it and sold it to the peddler, and now the magician wants it back."

"All right," said Ariel doubtfully. "But I don't see how you're going to convince

Andrina to give up the trunk, magician or no magician."

"Listen. First Gil and I dress up like a magician—a scary one," Marlon explained. "We'll need to gather a crowd of people somewhere near the palace, where Andrina is likely to hear what's going on.

"Then," Gil said, "we'll start asking questions about the princess who bought the trunk, and we'll send someone to fetch Andrina to come and see the magic show."

"You guys are going to do a magic show?" asked Ariel.

"Yeah," said Marlon. "I know a few tricks. But the best one will be the one we play on Andrina. . . ." Marlon, Gil, and Coral huddled around Ariel and explained the rest of the plan.

"Hmm," said Ariel when they were through. "It just might work. I'm sure my sisters will want to be in on this, too." She grinned. "After all, this is war!"

"Abracadabra! Alacazam!" shouted the strange and very tall magician who stood near the entrance to the palace. He waved his arms through the water in front of him, and a dozen tiny starfish floated from the wide sleeves of his glittering star-covered robe.

"Ooh!" murmured the small crowd that had gathered in front of the magician.

"Do another trick!" Flounder called out.

"No," boomed the magician. "I have come

to this sea in search of my lost possessions. Until I have recovered them, I cannot perform my magic show."

"What did you lose?" asked a small mermaid in the crowd.

"A trunk full of miracles!" cried the magician dramatically. His long white hair floated across his face.

"Where did you lose it?" Aquata called out.

"It was stolen from me in a far-off sea," said the magician. "I found the thief, but he had already sold it to an honest old peddler woman."

"A peddler woman was here in the kingdom not long ago," said Alana.

"So I've heard," said the magician. He pulled a magic wand from his sleeve and began to wave it. "I sense that the trunk is very near."

"But the peddler woman is gone," cried Ariel. "How can the trunk be near here?" The crowd around the magician was growing. Ariel noticed that Andrina had come out of the castle and was watching from a short distance.

"Can your magic find the trunk?" Adella called out.

"Someone in this city has it," said the magician. He pulled a small crystal ball from his other sleeve and held it out in front of him. Gazing at the ball, he chanted the magic words again. "Abracadabra! Alacazam! I see the trunk. It is very near indeed. In fact, it is in that very castle!" The magician pointed at the castle. The crowd murmured.

Ariel noticed that Andrina had moved into the crowd and was standing a few feet away from the magician.

"The trunk is in the possession of a princess of this realm!" The magician waved his hand over the crystal ball. He peered into it closely, then began to chant once again. "Abracadabra! Alacazam! Is that the one?" the magician shouted, pointing to Andrina. "You are the princess who has my stolen property!"

"Stolen property?" Andrina repeated. "What are you talking about? I didn't steal anything."

"You have my trunk!"

"I have *a* trunk," answered Andrina cautiously. "But I bought it from a peddler."

"But you must realize by now that it was not hers to sell. You must realize that it belongs to me, a powerful magician. Do you think such a collection of treasures is simply meant for the amusement of a young girl?"

"Maybe I did buy a trunk," said Andrina defensively. "But that still doesn't necessarily mean it's the one you lost."

Ariel stifled a giggle at the worried look on Andrina's face. Marlon really had her fooled!

"That trunk is mine," said the magician. "And I can prove it."

"How?" asked Andrina. She didn't want to give up the trunk. There were still so many things in it she hadn't used. But if it really belonged to someone else, she knew she would have to return it.

"Does this look familiar?" The magician held up a huge glittering jewel.

"Well, yes," said Andrina. "I had one just like it in the trunk. Just because you have one, too, that doesn't prove anything."

"Take it," said the magician. "Open it."

"Oh, I already know what will happen," Andrina replied with a giggle. "Eels pop out, right?" She pressed the button, obviously expecting the fake eels to explode out. Instead, a cloud of dark purple squid ink spread out of the jewel so quickly that Andrina didn't have time to move away. The next thing she knew, the cloud of ink had washed across her, staining her face and body.

"Hey, look—she turned purple!" cried a little merboy in the crowd. The princesses all began to laugh. Even Marlon couldn't hold back a chuckle.

"What!" sputtered Andrina. "How dare you!"

"I think it suits you," said Aquata. "Purple definitely looks better on you than on me."

"If you want the antidote to that ink," said the magician, "I'm afraid you'll have to give me back my trunk."

"That's a mean trick!" cried Andrina. "I bought that trunk fair and square."

"Fine," said the magician. "Keep the trunk.

And be the purple princess from now on."
Everyone began to laugh—everyone except
Andrina, that is.

"Oh, all right," she said angrily. "If you're
going to be that way about it, you can have
your silly trunk back. But first make this
purple stuff go away."

"No, the trunk first," said the magician.

"If you insist," she said. She stormed back
into the palace, her tail swishing angrily. A
few moments later she returned, dragging
the trunk behind her. Dover the butler
hurried after her, trying to help, but she
brushed him away impatiently.

"There," she said, dropping the trunk in
front of the magician. "Now, if you don't
mind?"

"Oh, yes," said the magician. "Just use a
little ordinary soap. It comes right off with
that."

"Soap!" Andrina was stunned. "I can't
believe it!"

"If you think that's hard to believe, see if
you can believe this!" said Gil, swimming
out from beneath the robe as Marlon grinned
and pulled off the long white wig. Andrina

stared in disbelief for a second before she realized that the magician wasn't a tall white-haired man after all.

"Marlon and Gil!" Andrina gasped. She looked around at her sisters and Coral, who were laughing hard. "This was all a joke!" She stared at them. Gradually her expression changed from anger and confusion to amusement. She began to laugh. "Good one, guys!"

"We couldn't let you go on the way you were with your practical jokes," said Ariel. "We thought this was a better solution than telling Daddy."

"But how did you know about the trunk?" Andrina asked.

"When he heard about all your props, Marlon guessed that you had bought it from the peddler," Coral explained.

Andrina looked around at her sisters and friends. Everyone seemed to be waiting for her to say something. "Well, I guess this is supposed to have taught me a lesson," she said.

The sisters all glared at her. "We certainly hope so," said Aquata.

"OK, OK," Andrina said. "I'm sorry about

what happened with the oysters yesterday, Alana. I guess I just didn't realize it would upset you so much." She turned to her youngest sister. "And Ariel, like I said before, I'm sorry my trick ruined your science project. I really will help you redo it, I promise."

"Thanks," said Ariel. She grinned at Coral, Marlon, and Gil. "And don't worry, Andrina. We'll hold you to that promise."

"Well?" Adella demanded when Andrina didn't say anything else. "Don't you have some apologies for the rest of us?"

"No way," Andrina replied with a laugh. "The rest of my jokes turned out great!" When her sisters continued to glare at her, Andrina finally relented. "All right, you win. I guess I got kind of carried away there for a while. But does this mean I can't ever play another joke?"

"No, of course not," said Aquata. "But it does mean that you're going to give the contents of that mysterious trunk to Gil and Marlon."

"Good idea," said Ariel. "I think they've earned it."

Andrina let out a long, dejected sigh. "Well, all right, if you insist. . . ."

"We do," said Attina quickly. She glanced at the boys. "You guys had better get this trunk emptied out before she changes her mind or gets any more crazy ideas."

Gil and Marlon didn't need to be told twice. They eagerly began pulling things out of the trunk, arguing good-naturedly about who got what. When the trunk was almost empty Andrina shooed them away and closed the lid. "That's enough, you two. You have to leave me *some* ammunition." Before anyone could object to that, she threw her arms around the sisters nearest to her and gave them a big hug. "I *am* sorry, you guys. I promise I won't let my joking get so crazy again. Come on, let's all go out for something to eat." The others began to laugh again.

"Maybe you should wash up first," Ariel suggested.

Andrina began to laugh, too. She had forgotten about turning purple. "Good idea," she said.

"And listen, Andrina," said Adella, "no hard feelings, OK?" She stuck out her hand for her sister to shake. But when Andrina took it, she jumped in surprise as a device hidden in Adella's palm let off a loud noise like the hiss of an angry eel.

"Eek!" Andrina cried. Then she started to laugh again. "I'll get you back for that one, Adella," she said.

"Oh no!" her sisters cried in dismay.

Andrina gave them a wink. "Just joking!"